In Memory of

MARIE TURISSINI BROWNING

© DEMCO, INC. 1990 PRINTED IN U.S.A.

12-8-98

POPPA'S ITCHY CHRISTMAS

Angela Shelf Medearis

illustrated by John Ward

Holiday House / New York

As soon as a little pink daylight broke through the darkness, I was up shouting "Merry Christmas! Merry Christmas!" Poppa came running into the room pulling his overalls over his nightshirt. He loves Christmas as much as I do. Grandma Tiny was right behind him. I had to shake Aunt Viney and Big Mama to wake them up. They're from Kansas City and are only visiting us for the holidays.

"All right, George," Big Mama grumbled. "We're awake. I'll be in there as soon as I find my specs."

Aunt Viney mumbled something into her pillow. I didn't wait around to find out what it was. When they finally came into the front room, we all exchanged gifts. I'd been squeezing and shaking those pretty green and red boxes for more than a week.

My gift from Aunt Viney was in a long, narrow box. I was hoping it was a BB gun. It wasn't. Instead, it was the longest, ugliest muffler I'd ever seen, with more colors in it than a rainbow. All I could do was stare at it.

"What do you say, George?" demanded Grandma Tiny.

"Thank you, Aunt Viney," I mumbled.

"You're welcome, baby! Merry Christmas," said Aunt Viney.

Next, I opened the present from Big Mama. It was wrapped up in beautiful red-and-gold paper and looked about the right size for a baseball glove. When I unwrapped it, I was so disappointed I could have cried. Underwear. The reddest, itchiest, woolliest pair of long underwear I'd ever seen. I caught a glimpse of Poppa's face. He was holding up a pair of long red underwear, too.

Poppa winked at me and I felt a little better. I opened his and Grandma Tiny's gift last. I'd already been wrong twice, so I didn't even try to guess what was in their box. A pair of ice skates! They were just what I'd asked for! I hugged Poppa and Grandma Tiny and told them they were the best grandparents in the whole wide world.

"Make sure that pond is frozen solid before you try to skate on it, George," Poppa warned. "Sometimes looks are deceiving."

"I'll be careful, Poppa," I said.

Everyone loved my gifts. The womenfolk went on and on about the bookmarks I'd made them. Poppa told me his new shaving mug was just what he'd been hoping for.

Poppa and I cleared away the boxes and wrapping paper. Grandma Tiny, Big Mama, and Aunt Viney began stirring, tasting, and seasoning enormous pots of food. Soon the house smelled like every good thing that had ever been grown on earth.

The aroma of baked goose steamed out of the oven. A clove-studded ham lay in slices on the chopping board. Plump, juicy apple pies, mincemeat pies, pumpkin pies laced with cinnamon, cakes with glaze, and tins of sugar cookies were locked up in the pie safe. Our house and our stomachs were going to be full to bursting this day.

"Poppa," Grandma Tiny called out. "I believe we're going to need a little more wood before everything's said and done."

Poppa groaned. "Tiny honey," he said. "I thought I brought in enough wood last night."

"Well," said Grandma Tiny. "You thought wrong. All this cooking is taking a heap of kindling."

"Honey," said Poppa, rubbing his joints. "I've got the misery in my knees from doing all this work. Where's George?"

"I don't know where that boy is," Grandma Tiny said. "George! Go chop us some more wood, please. *Geoooorge!*" Grandma Tiny sang out my name like a champion hog caller.

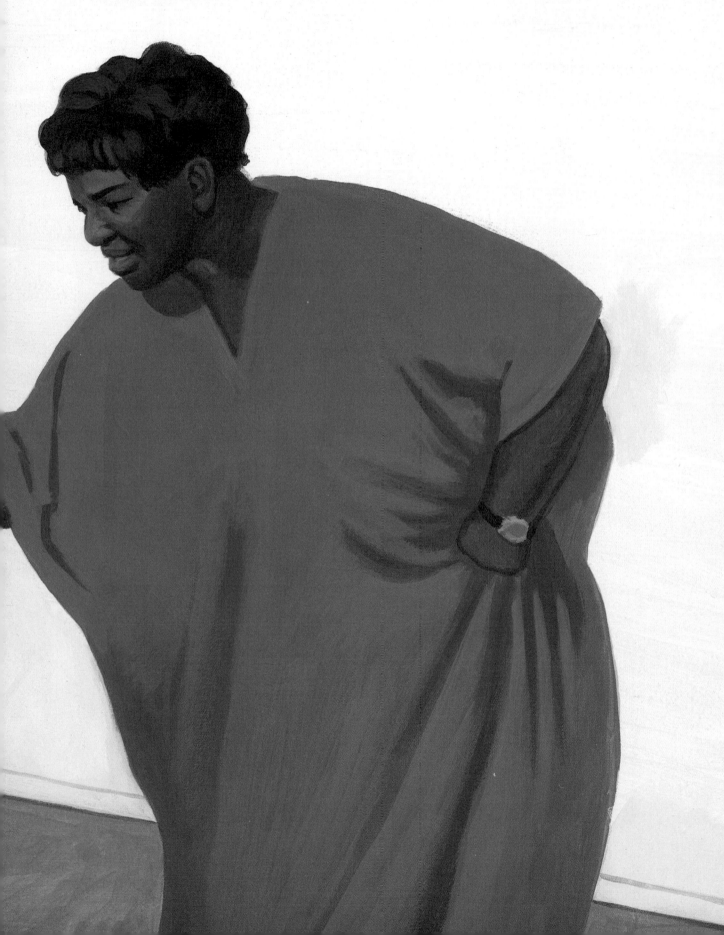

I had just gotten comfortable underneath my grandparents' four-poster bed. It was the perfect place to hide from a group of wild women, or so I thought. I was about to eat a slice of ham I'd grabbed, when Big Mama hauled me out from under there like a sack of potatoes. I crammed the meat into my mouth as fast as I could.

"There you are!" Big Mama said. "I saw your foot sticking out. Didn't you hear your grandma calling you?"

"Mm, mm," I mumbled.

"Speak up, boy, I can't hear you," Big Mama said. "We need more wood. But before you go out, put on your new long johns. They'll keep you warm." She smiled. "It's so cold out today, my false teeth froze while they were soaking."

I swallowed and said, "Oh, I'll be all right, Big Mama."

"No sir," said Big Mama. "You march right in there and put them on. I want to make sure they fit."

It was no use arguing. I went in my room and put on the long johns.

"They're a little long," I said.

"They'll do," Big Mama said as she looked me over. "You're going to think it's a hot day in June with those on."

"Yes ma'am," I said miserably. They were hot all right. I was itching in places I had never itched before. I couldn't wait to finish chopping that wood so I could get out of that long underwear. I grabbed my jacket off the hook, but before I could go outside, I ran into Aunt Viney.

"There you are," she said smiling. "I was just looking for you. We need some more wood."

"Yes ma'am," I said. "I was just fixing to go and get some more."

"It's plum freezing outside," Aunt Viney said. "Almost cold enough to freeze air into ice cubes. Here, I found the muffler I made for you stuffed behind a chair. I wonder how it got there."

"That's strange," I said. I should have hidden that thing in the cellar. It was too late now.

"Oh well," Aunt Viney said. "I'm sure glad I found it." She wrapped it around and around my neck like it was a multicolored boa constrictor. Then she crossed the rest of the scarf over my chest. There was still a lot left over, so she wrapped it under my arms twice and crossed the ends over my chest again. I could barely button my jacket. My arms stuck out stiffly on either side.

"Thank you, Aunt Viney," I said.

"You're welcome, baby."

I pulled open the back door. "George," Grandma Tiny hollered from the kitchen. "Just where do you think you're going without your boots? Do you want to catch your death? It's so cold that when I set the milk pitcher near the window it turned into vanilla ice cream."

I laughed and looked in the closet for my things. I found my boots and put them on. My new skates were right next to my boots. I slung the skates over my shoulder. Maybe the pond was frozen and I could skate after cutting the firewood.

The wood pile near the barn had only a few scrawny pieces of wood left. All the logs were gone. I remembered that a tree over near the pond had been struck down by lightning. I could take my sled and chop enough wood from the tree to hold us for a while. Then I'd have a chance to try out my new skates before hauling the wood back. I shouldered my ax, got my sled, and took the snow-covered path into the woods.

I found the fallen tree and started cutting off its branches. Even though it was cold, I was sweating because of all the clothes I was wearing. I took off my muffler, my jacket, and my flannel shirt and hung them on a tree branch. Even without them, I was still warm because of that heavy-duty red underwear.

I stacked the cut wood on the sled. Then I put on my skates. The frozen pond glittered like a diamond in the sun. I stomped on it a little bit. It seemed solid.

I glided out and did a few figure eights. I'd almost skated to the middle when I heard a cracking sound. The ice wasn't solid. It was giving way!

My heart pounded in my ears. I tried to get back to solid ground. My legs flopped under me like a newborn colt's. The ice broke a little more with every step I took. I couldn't seem to move fast enough. I wasn't far from the bank when the ice splintered like broken glass. I plunged right through it into the water.

The freezing water took my breath away. My neck snapped back and I hit my head on the edge of the ice. Something kept me from sinking, but I couldn't figure out what. I began to shake all over.

"Help, help," I screamed. "Somebody help me." I called and called until my throat was hoarse.

I must have passed out because, all of a sudden, I heard Poppa yelling my name.

"Grab the end, George," Poppa said. "Then I'll pull you out." Poppa was lying flat on his stomach on the edge of the bank. He had a rock tied to the end of my muffler. He slid it across the ice. It slithered toward me in a rainbow blur of color. I grabbed it. Poppa pulled me out of the water and onto the bank.

I don't know how we made it home. The next thing I knew, Grandma Tiny, Aunt Viney, and Big Mama were fluttering around the foot of my bed. They were acting like three nervous hens at Sunday dinnertime.

"Cover him with blankets," Grandma Tiny ordered.

"Put a mustard plaster on his chest," said Aunt Viney.

"Soak his feet in hot water and Epsom's salts," hollered Big Mama.

"Make some hot tea! Dose him with Black Draught! Where's the Cod Liver Oil?" They were all fussing at once.

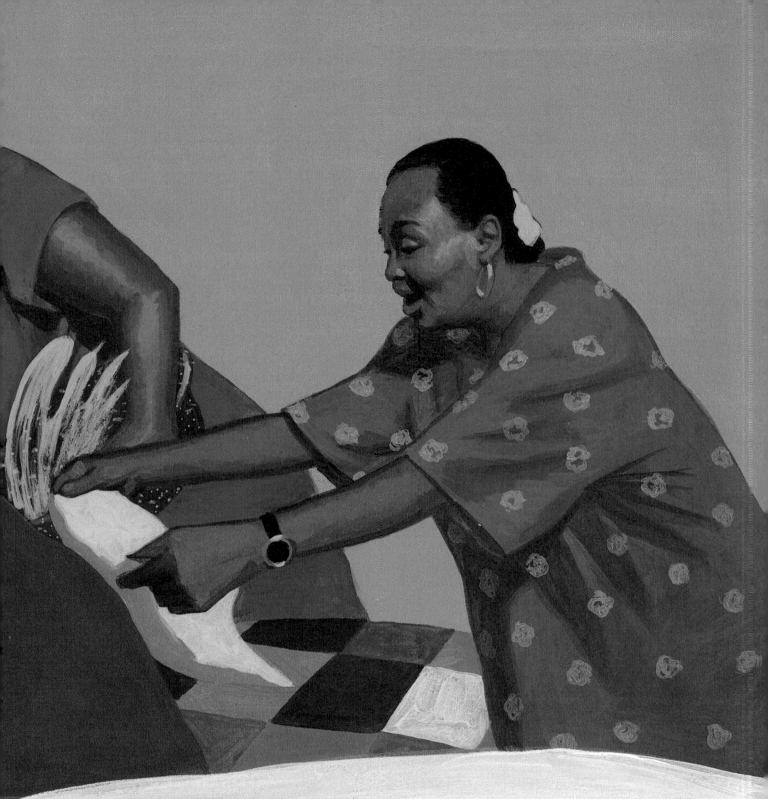

"Tiny, Viney, and Big Mama!" Poppa shouted. "That's enough of that racket! Ain't that much wrong with this boy. He wasn't in the water that long and all he's got is a bump on his head. You had enough clothes on him to smother an elephant. Why don't you just let him rest?"

Grandma Tiny, Aunt Viney, and Big Mama closed their mouths with a snap. Poppa hardly ever raised his voice. Their eyes looked as if they'd pop out of their heads. One by one they backed out of the room.

"Go to sleep now, George," Poppa said. He patted my cheek and followed them out of the room.

I don't know how long I slept, but when I woke up everyone was eating Christmas dinner. I eased out of bed and got Poppa's attention.

"Poppa," I said. "I'm powerful hungry."

"Get back into bed and I'll fix you up a plate," Poppa said. "Your grandma saved a drumstick for you."

I looked out the window for a while. A big round moon was shining on the snow. The pond looked cold and scary. The ice glittered like a cat's eyes in the dark.

Poppa came in with a heaping plate of food on a tray. "Hop up into bed now, George."

"Poppa," I said, "I've had a mighty strange Christmas."

"That sure is the truth," Poppa said. "But I'm mighty grateful for your new red underwear and muffler."

I nearly choked on my food. "Why?"

Poppa smiled. "If your underwear hadn't gotten hooked on a piece of ice, you would have drowned. I've fallen in love with mine, even though it makes me itch all over." We both laughed.

"And without that extra long muffler, I wouldn't have been able to pull you out of the pond," Poppa said.

"I guess they were good gifts after all," I said.

"They sure were," Poppa agreed.

"Looks like the present I wanted got me into trouble," I said. "And the presents I hated saved my life."

"That's about the size of it, George," Poppa said.

"Thank you for everything, Poppa," I said. I saluted him with my drumstick.

"You're welcome, George," Poppa said. "Merry Christmas."

To Mrs. Kaye Dunn and all the
wonderful students, teachers, and librarians in Austin, Texas.
A. S. M.

To John C. Ward, Sr., my dad
J. W., Jr.

Text copyright © 1998 by Angela Shelf Medearis
Illustrations copyright © 1998 by John Ward
ALL RIGHTS RESERVED
Printed in the United States of America
FIRST EDITION

Library of Congress Cataloging-in-Publication Data
Medearis, Angela Shelf, 1956–
Poppa's itchy Christmas / by Angela Shelf Medearis; illustrated
by John Ward. — 1st ed.
p.   cm.
Summary: George is unhappy to receive a homemade muffler and itchy
long underwear for Christmas, but they come in handy when he has an
accident while ice skating.
ISBN 0-8234-1298-9
[1. Christmas—Fiction.   2. Gifts—Fiction.   3. Clothing and
dress—Fiction.   4. Ice skating—Fiction.]   I. Ward, John (John
Clarence), ill.   II. Title.
PZ7.M51274Pk   1998   96-40170   CIP
[Fic]—dc21   AC